Ace of Wands

A FATED LOVERS SHORT PARANORMAL, TAROT ROMANCE

TAROT FANTASIES
BOOK EIGHT

JAX WILDER

Ace of Wands

Tarot Fantasies Series

Jax Wilder

RAINBOW QUARTZ PUBLISHING

Published by Rainbow Quartz Publishing

Edmonds WA, 98026

ISBN: 978-1-961714-51-9 First Edition: 2024

Cover design by Miranda Townsend

Interior design by Miranda Townsend

Tarot Card description by Lorelai Hamilton from the book Teenage Tarot – used with permission.

This book is a work of fiction. Names, characters, places, and incidents are either the product of the author's imagination or used fictitiously. Any resemblance to actual events, locales, or persons, living or dead, is entirely coincidental.

For permissions or inquiries, please contact:

Rainbow Quartz Publishing

rainbowquartzpublishing@gmail.com www.RQPublishing.com

To those living with unseen disabilities, this one is for you.

For the silent warriors who navigate a world that doesn't always understand, who face challenges invisible to the eye but felt deeply within. Your strength, resilience, and courage inspire more than you know. May this story remind you that your life is full of possibilities, that you are worthy of love, adventure, and joy—just as you are.

This book is a tribute to your journey, and a reminder that you are never alone.

Jai Wilder

Ace of Wands

"The world is full of possibilities — what are you waiting for?" Ace of Wands.

Key Words and Phrases
New beginnings and opportunities
Creativity and inspiration
Potential and growth
Taking initiative and action
Passion and enthusiasm
Igniting a spark or fire within
Manifesting goals and desires
Confidence and assertiveness
Energy and vitality
Boldness and courage to pursue dreams

T he Ace of Wands card is like a burst of energy and creativity—it's all about new beginnings and exciting opportunities.

There's a hand reaching out from the clouds, holding a wand with leaves sprouting from it. The universe is calling to you. Here's your chance to ignite your passions and start something new.

The Ace of Wands is about dreaming—it's also about taking action. Don't just sit back and wait for things to happen. Get out there and make them happen.

—Lorelai Hamilton, author of *Teenage Tarot* and *Tarot Tales & Magic Spells*

ACE of WANDS.

Chapter One

There is this recurring dream I had where I walked along a sandy beach while the sun kissed my skin. The warmth burrowed deep into my bones, into the very fiber of my being. But it was only ever a dream because if I walked along that beach in reality, the sun could kill me.

The dream always felt so real. I could hear the waves crashing against the shore, feel the gritty sand beneath my feet, and smell the salty air as it tangled in my hair. The sun warmed my skin like a comforting embrace, a sensation I had craved my whole life but never truly experienced. Most people were afraid of the dark, but I was afraid of the sun.

I woke up from this dream countless times, the reality of my condition settling over me like a cold shadow. My skin, sensitive to even the smallest amount of UV radiation, kept me confined to the safety of darkness. I liked to joke that I was a vampire, a creature of the night, unable to face the sun. But even vampires got to roam freely during the night without fear of the sun's betrayal come morning.

In a small town like Coral Cove, everyone knew me as "the girl who can't go out during the day." Children dared each other to touch the door of my house, the door of the "vampire" of Coral Cove. It wasn't exactly the kind of notoriety I wanted. Still, it was what it was. Most folks around there were kind and understanding. They didn't stare too long, and they tried not to ask too many questions, though I could see the pity in their eyes.

My life was a delicate dance between the shadows and the moonlight. It was a lonely existence sometimes, but I had learned to find beauty in the night, the same way others found it in the daylight. I had made a life for myself, and while it could feel isolating, it was still fulfilling.

Mostly.

I worked from home as an accountant, crunching the numbers by the light of my computer screen while the world slept. My family visited me in the evenings, and my friends were more than willing to accommodate my unique schedule. Plus, video messaging had really taken off in the last few years. I had everything I needed.

Everything except for the sun.

That night, like so many nights before, I wandered through the quiet streets of Coral Cove, the air crisp with the scent of the ocean. It was nearly midnight, and the world was asleep, save for the faint hum of distant waves and the occasional rustle of leaves in the breeze. The stars were scattered like diamonds across the black velvet sky, a sight so magnificent it almost made up for the sun I would never see.

The Arcane Room stood on the corner of Water Street, a small shop with an aura of mystery and enchantment. Its windows glowed with a soft, inviting light that spilled onto the sidewalk, and the sign above the door swung gently in the night breeze.

I had always felt a strange, comforting pull to this place. The scent of incense wafted out as I pushed the door open, mingling with the aroma of herbs and candles. The shop was a treasure trove of curiosities, filled with shelves of crystals, tarot cards, and other esoteric items that seemed to whisper stories of their own.

Ms. Vesper stood behind the counter, her eyes twinkling with otherworldly knowledge. She was an enigma, wrapped in colorful scarves and adorned with jewelry that jingled softly with her every movement. "Evening, Clark," she greeted me with a warm smile, her voice as soothing as the night itself. "Aren't you a ravishing goddess this evening."

My cheeks warmed. "Stop it, you know I'm more of a demigoddess anyway," I winked. "Thanks for opening for me. I really appreciate it," I said.

"Always," she said with a smile. "I have work to do anyway, and it's always easier at night with no one to disturb me."

I smiled, but I knew it didn't reach my eyes.

"What brings you in tonight?" Ms. Vesper asked.

"I'm running low on candles," I replied, wandering through the aisles, my fingers trailing along the smooth surface of various trinkets. "I thought it was time for a restock."

Candles were my constant companions. They bathed my home in soft light and provided the kind of warmth I could only dream of feeling from the sun. They made the darkness feel a little less daunting.

Ms. Vesper nodded, understanding in her gaze. "Candles, of course. And maybe something a little extra?"

I raised an eyebrow, intrigued. "What do you mean? Did you have something in mind?"

She beckoned me closer, her eyes gleaming. "I have some special items that I only share with the most coveted of customers. Things that might interest someone like you—someone with a penchant for dreams and the night."

Curiosity piqued, I followed her to a small table adorned with a rich tapestry. Upon it rested a deck of tarot cards, their intricate designs hinting at untold stories. Ms. Vesper gestured to the deck. "Why not draw a card? See what the night holds for you."

I hesitated for a moment, then reached out and drew a card from the deck. It was the Ace of Wands. It looked kind of depressing, if I was being honest with myself. I tried not to roll my eyes.

Ms. Vesper leaned closer, her voice a whisper of secrets. "The Ace of Wands is a card of inspiration and new beginnings," she said, pointing to the vibrant, blossoming wand on the card. "This wand represents the spark of creativity and the potential for growth. It's a reminder that within you lies the power to ignite new passions and pursue your dreams with renewed energy. The world is full of possibilities, and this card encourages you to seize them."

Her words resonated within me as I studied the card, the image a powerful reminder of untapped potential and the exciting paths that lay ahead. It wasn't just a promise of something more—it was an invitation to take hold of my destiny and shape it with my own hands.

"Come with me," Ms. Vesper said. She led me to a room in the back of the shop. The inside was white, with a single black leather chaise lounge. "Have a seat, Clark, and drink this." She offered me a cup of tea, a fragrant blend that soothed my senses. "Just relax. I promise, no matter how much time it feels like you've spent here, only twenty minutes will pass."

My body tensed at the thought of sleeping and staying out past sunrise. Doing so could cause neurodegeneration and skin cancer.

"Do you trust me?" Ms. Vesper asked.

I looked into her eyes and found that I did. I nodded, sat back, and took a sip of the warm tea. The world around me began to blur, the shop's edges softening as if dissolving into a dream. I closed my eyes. When I opened them again, I found myself standing on the sunlit beach from my dreams.

The sand was warm beneath my feet, the waves singing their eternal song. The sun kissed my skin with a gentle caress, and for a moment, I was free, unburdened by the chains of reality.

A figure emerged from the surf, his silhouette a striking contrast against the sky. I took a deep breath, the air filled with possibility. Here, in this dream, the sun was no longer my enemy. In the quiet heart of Coral Cove, beneath the moon's watchful gaze, I began to believe in the impossible.

My skin was kissed by the sun.

Chapter Two

There was a long moment after I opened my eyes when I forgot I had XP. It was a glorious moment when I felt normal, when xeroderma pigmentosum wasn't my defining characteristic. The brightness was overwhelming, and I instinctively raised my arms to shield my face. Panic surged through me as my mind screamed danger. I had spent my entire life fearing the sun, knowing its rays could burn my skin and destroy me in moments.

I stumbled backward, expecting pain, expecting to feel my skin blistering under the sun's assault. All it would take was a few minutes in the sun, and I'd forfeit my life to a painful, cancer-riddled ending. But instead, there was only warmth—a gentle, comforting heat that wrapped around me like a soft blanket. I lowered my arms and blinked against the sunlight, trying to make sense of what I was seeing.

The beach stretched out before me, an endless expanse of golden sand and rolling waves. The air was salty and sweet, and the sky was an endless blue that seemed to go on forever. It was the dream.

This was a dream.

I was in The Arcane Room.

I took a tentative step forward, the sand warm beneath my feet. I was standing in the sun, and I was perfectly fine.

"It's okay," a voice said from behind me. I turned to see a man emerging from the surf, water dripping from his long dark hair and glistening on his tanned skin. He looked like he belonged here, like he was a part of this sunlit world I had only dreamed of. "You're safe here."

"Who are you?" I asked, my voice barely above a whisper.

He smiled, a grin as bright as the sun itself. "I'm Kade. Welcome to your dream, Clark. This is a place created by the Arcane Room. Here, you're free."

My heart hammered in my chest, a mix of fear and disbelief. "This is impossible," I said, shaking my head. "The sun... I can't be in the sun."

Kade stepped closer, his eyes gentle and reassuring. "In this world, you can. Here, the rules are different. The Arcane Room lets you live out your dreams without limits."

His words washed over me, calming the fear that had gripped me. Despite everything I knew, everything I had been told my entire life, I felt a strange sense of safety. I was standing in the sun, and nothing was hurting me.

I took a deep breath, filling my lungs with the salty air. For the first time, I allowed myself to truly feel the sun on my skin, its warmth sinking into my bones and melting away the shadows that had been my constant companions.

"Come on," Kade said, nodding toward the water.

I hesitated for a moment, then followed him toward the waves. Each step felt like a victory, a defiance of the boundaries my condition had imposed on me. The ocean lapped at my feet, cool and refreshing, and I felt a laugh bubbling up inside me.

"This is unbelievable," I said, blinking back tears of joy.

Kade chuckled. "It's your dream, Clark. You can have anything you want here."

We walked along the shoreline, the sand warm and soft beneath our feet. Kade pointed out seashells and pieces of driftwood, his enthusiasm contagious. The fear that had gripped me slowly ebbed away, replaced with a sense of freedom.

As we wandered, my thoughts drifted to my past. Memories of a relationship that once seemed so promising but ended in heartbreak. My ex made it clear that my condition was too much for him to handle. He left me while sitting next to me, the emotional cavern between us too big to bridge. It left me feeling broken. I vowed then that I didn't need anyone, that I could live a fulfilling life on my own.

But here, in this dream world where the sun kissed my skin without consequence, I allowed myself to imagine something different.

"Kade," I said, glancing at him. "Do you really think I can have anything I want here?"

"I know so," he said with a crooked grin and a wink. "Here, you're in control."

"It's all like a dream, right?"

Kade nodded slowly. "Your body is safe while you are here. And some might describe this as a dream."

"A dream that feels so real."

Kade chuckled, a deep throaty laugh. "Yes, it sure can."

I leaned into the newfound confidence coursing through my veins, and I reached for his hand, lacing my fingers between Kade's. "Anything?"

He rubbed my thumb with his own. "Your wildest dreams."

"Then I want you," I said, my voice steady and sure. "Outside, under the sun."

A wicked smile played across his lips as he led me to a spot on the beach. There was a blanket spread out on the sand. The sun shone down on us, and for the first time in ages, I felt truly alive.

"Can you make anything happen here?"

"You can make anything happen. Dream it, baby."

"I would love a margarita and one of those fancy loungers."

Kade only smiled.

When I glanced back at the blanket, there wasn't just a margarita; there was a table with ten flavors of fruity slushy drinks, each equipped with an adorable umbrella.

"Perhaps a bed on the beach would be nicer. Something with lots of pillows," I said, testing what I could conjure.

Instantly, the blanket and lounger were replaced with a luxurious round bed. The pillows and blankets made it seem like stepping not just into a magical realm but into paradise itself.

I walked around the bed, running my fingers along the fabrics, and selected a fancy blue drink to sip. If real life could only be so simple.

Kade still glistened with the salty seawater. His sun-kissed skin glowed.

"Can I have a towel?" I asked, motioning for him to come closer.

He stepped forward, water droplets glistening on his chest. I took a towel from the bed and slowly, deliberately, began drying him off. My fingers glided over the hard planes of his muscles, tracing each contour, memorizing the feel of him beneath my touch.

Kade watched me, his gaze heated, but he said nothing, allowing me to take the lead. I savored the control, the power I held in this dream world. Here, I wasn't sick, I was the one in charge. Here, I could have what I wanted, and right then, I wanted him.

I tossed the towel aside, letting my hands explore his chest, feeling the steady beat of his heart beneath my palm. Kade's breath hitched, and I smiled, knowing that I was the one making him feel this way.

"Lie down," I said softly, and he obeyed without question, reclining on the bed, his eyes locked on mine.

I climbed onto the bed, straddling him, my hands still roaming over his body. The sun bathed us in its warm, golden light, and I felt invincible, like nothing could touch me here.

Kade's hands rested on my hips, his grip firm but not controlling. He was letting me set the pace, letting me take what I wanted. And what I wanted was him—all of him.

I leaned down, my lips brushing against his ear. "You're mine, Kade. In this world, you belong to me."

A low growl rumbled in his chest, but it was a sound of approval, of desire. "All yours, Clark. I'm here to serve you, to please only you."

With that, I captured his lips in a fierce, demanding kiss. It was a kiss that spoke of longing, of years spent in the shadows, and of finally stepping into the light. Kade responded with equal fervor, his hands sliding up my back, pulling me closer.

I straddled him, feeling the hard planes of his chest beneath my fingertips as I traced slow, deliberate lines over his skin. Beneath me, I could feel his erection straining against his shorts, pressing into me. The warmth pooled in my center, spreading through me like a wildfire. My breath quickened as I lowered my lips to his, tasting the salt of the sea mixed with the sweetness of his mouth. Our tongues danced together, a heated exchange that left me breathless.

Kade's hands moved to my hips, gripping me firmly as I rocked against his refection that strained against his shorts. The friction sending waves of pleasure through my body. I broke the kiss, my lips hovering just above his, and whispered, "I want you on top of me."

With a swift, powerful movement, Kade flipped us over, his body pressing me into the softness of the bed. He gazed down at me, his eyes dark with desire as he slowly peeled my clothes away, piece by piece, until I was naked under the sun. The sunlight kissed every inch of my bare skin, a sensation so foreign yet so utterly intoxicating.

"Tell me what you want," he murmured, his voice husky with need.

I pointed to my collarbone, tracing a line down to my chest. "Kiss me here," I commanded.

Kade followed the path I traced, his lips trailing heated kisses along my skin, sending shivers of pleasure through my body. When he reached my breasts, he took one nipple between his fingers, pinching and rolling it gently. The jolt of pleasure that shot through me to my center made my back arch, a soft moan escaping my lips.

"More," I whispered, my voice trembling with need. "I want you to taste me… eat me until I scream."

His eyes darkened further as he slid down my body, spreading my legs with gentle, insistent hands. He started with fervent kisses at my hips, then my inner thighs, making his way closer to where I ached for him most. When his tongue finally slid over my wet slit, I gasped, my fingers tangling in his hair as he licked from my entrance to my clit, slow and deliberate.

"You taste so good," he murmured against me, his breath warm and teasing. "Like honey and apples."

I pulled him up just enough to meet his gaze. "I want a taste," I said, my voice a low purr.

Kade slipped a finger inside me, curling it just right before pulling it out, slick with my juices. He brought the finger to my lips, and I took it in, sucking it slowly. The taste was pleasantly sweet, a reminder of the desire coursing through my veins.

I released his finger with a soft pop. "Now go back to pleasuring me."

Kade grinned wickedly before lowering himself again, his tongue delving deep into my folds, tasting every curve, exploring every inch of me with a hunger that matched my own. He found my clit and focused on it, licking and sucking in a rhythm that had me panting, my body coiled tight with pleasure.

As his tongue worked its magic, I couldn't help but think back to the only other person who had tried to taste me. He had gagged, leaving me feeling ugly, like something was wrong with me. But with Kade, I realized it was never my problem—it was his. Kade couldn't get enough of me, and the way he devoured me only proved it.

When I finally came, it was like a thousand fireworks exploding inside me, every nerve ending igniting with pleasure. My entire body felt like it was set on fire, and I screamed with the intensity of it, my hands gripping the sheets as waves of ecstasy crashed over me.

The pleasure lingered, licking at my skin as I gasped for breath, my body trembling beneath the weight of what we had just shared. Kade moved up to hold me, his strong arms cradling me as I slowly came back down to earth.

The world around us faded away, leaving only

the two of us, entwined in the warmth of the sun and the heat of our passion. Here, in this dream, I was strong, I was in control, and I was free.

And for the first time in my life, I let myself truly believe that I deserved this happiness, that I deserved to take what I wanted, to live my life without limits.

Because in this world, anything was possible.

And right then, I wanted to be with Kade.

Chapter Three

As we lay together on the sun-drenched beach, the warmth of our passion still humming through my veins, I found myself craving more—more sun, more freedom, more experiences that I had only ever dreamed of. I turned to Kade, my fingers tracing lazy circles on his chest.

"Kade," I murmured, my voice still thick with satisfaction. "I want to feel the sun on my skin, as much of it as I can. I want to wear a sexy sundress, something barely there, something that lets me feel the warmth everywhere."

A slow, wicked smile spread across Kade's lips. "I can make that happen," he said, his voice a low rumble. With a wave of his hand, he conjured a sundress—a slinky, ethereal thing that seemed to be woven from sunlight itself.

The dress floated before me, delicate and nearly

transparent. The fabric was a soft, buttery yellow, the color of the sun just before it sets. It clung to the body in all the right places, with thin straps that would barely stay on my shoulders and a neckline that dipped low, teasing just enough to be tantalizing. The hem skimmed the tops of my thighs, swaying gently with every movement, and the material was so light it felt like wearing nothing at all.

I slipped into the dress, the fabric caressing my skin like a lover's touch. The warmth of the sun seeped through the material, kissing every inch of me, and I let out a sigh of pure contentment.

Kade's eyes darkened with appreciation as he looked me over. "You look incredible," he said, his voice husky. "What else do you want, Clark? This is your world."

I took a deep breath, my mind racing with possibilities. "I want to visit a boardwalk," I said, the idea forming as I spoke. "Something reminiscent of Coney Island. I want to experience the vibrancy of life, the joy of being around people, the freedom I've never had."

In an instant, the beach transformed, and we were standing on a bustling boardwalk. The air was filled with the mingled scents of saltwater, fried dough, and cotton candy. The sun beat down on us, warming the wooden planks beneath our feet, and around us, the world was alive with the sounds of laughter, the creaking of rides, and the distant call of seagulls.

I looked around in awe, taking it all in. The boardwalk stretched out before us, lined with colorful stalls and arcades. Brightly lit signs advertised games, fortune tellers, and food stands. The Ferris wheel spun lazily in the distance, its lights twinkling like stars even in the daytime.

Kade took my hand, leading me to a stand where we bought a fluffy cloud of pink cotton candy. The sweetness melted on my tongue, and I laughed, the sound bubbling up from somewhere deep inside me. We wandered through the crowds, playing games and soaking up the energy of the place.

After winning a ridiculous number of stuffed animals at the ring toss, Kade turned to me with a gleam in his eye. "How about a ride?" he asked, nodding toward the biggest roller coaster on the boardwalk.

I glanced up at the massive structure, its tracks twisting and turning high above us. The thought of riding it filled me with a thrill. "Let's do it," I said, my heart already racing.

We made our way to the roller coaster, the anticipation building with each step. The line moved quickly, and before I knew it, we were seated side by side in the front car. The lap bar came down with a click, securing us in place, but I noticed that there was just enough room for something more.

I looked at Kade, a mischievous grin spreading

across my face. "Kade," I whispered, leaning in close. "I want you to finger me while we're on the coaster."

His eyes widened slightly, but then that familiar wicked smile returned. "As you wish, Clark."

The ride began to move, the car jerking forward as it started its ascent up the first ramp. Kade's hand slipped under the hem of my sundress, his fingers trailing up my thighs, sending shivers through me. The climb was slow, the tension building with every inch we ascended. I could feel my heartbeat in my throat, a mix of excitement and desire.

When his fingers found my center, I gasped, my body already aching for his touch. He teased me, his fingers playing lightly over my clit, his touch gentle but insistent. The higher we climbed, the more the anticipation built, both from the ride and from the growing pleasure between my legs.

Just as we reached the crest of the first hill, poised at the top with the world spread out before us, Kade slipped two of his massive fingers inside me, his thumb pressing against my clit. I couldn't hold back the moan that escaped my lips, my body tightening around him as the roller coaster plunged down the first drop.

The world blurred around us as we hurtled down the track, the wind whipping through my hair. Kade's fingers moved in sync with the twists and turns of the ride, his thumb rubbing circles over my clit, driving me higher and higher. I gripped the lap bar with one hand, the other buried in Kade's hair as my hips rocked against his hand.

Each dip and turn of the roller coaster sent jolts of pleasure through me, the adrenaline of the ride mingling with the growing pressure in my core. The sensation was overwhelming, a mix of fear and ecstasy that made my head spin. I could feel myself hurtling toward the edge, every nerve ending alive with sensation.

As we climbed the final hill, I was panting, my body on the brink. Kade's fingers curled inside me, hitting just the right spot, and as the coaster dropped for the final descent, I exploded. Pleasure rippled through me in waves, my body convulsing as I screamed out, the sound lost in the roar of the wind and the rush of the ride.

The world fell away, leaving nothing but the intense pleasure coursing through me, every nerve alight, every sensation magnified. My hands flew into the air, the force of my orgasm so powerful it left me trembling, tears of pure bliss streaming down my face.

As the coaster slowed to a stop, I collapsed back into the seat, breathless and spent, my body still humming with the aftershocks of my climax. Kade withdrew his hand, his fingers slick with my release, and he brought them to his lips, licking them clean with a satisfied grin.

"Delicious," he murmured, his voice low and rough with desire.

I laughed, the sound a mix of exhilaration and disbelief. "That was… incredible."

Kade leaned in, brushing his lips against mine in a soft, lingering kiss. "Anything is possible here, Clark," he whispered, his breath warm against my skin. "And there's so much more to experience."

I smiled, my heart still racing. In this world, I was free. I was alive. And I couldn't wait to see what came next.

Chapter Four

T he amusement park was alive with bright lights and the distant sound of laughter, a world of excitement beneath the darkened sky. The scent of popcorn and cotton candy filled the air, mingling with the salty breeze from the ocean. It was a place of joy, of carefree delight, but I had something else in mind today.

Kade and I had just stepped off a roller coaster, the adrenaline still pumping through my veins. My heart raced not just from the thrill of the ride but from the way Kade's hand lingered on the small of my back, his touch sending shivers down my spine.

I turned to him, eyes gleaming with determination. "Kade, I want to feel you inside me," I said, my voice low and breathless. "I want to know what your cock feels like."

His eyes darkened with desire, a slow smile

spreading across his lips. "You'll get exactly what you want," he promised, his voice a husky whisper that sent a wave of heat through me.

He took my hand, leading me through the throngs of people, past the carousel and the bumper cars, to the towering Ferris wheel at the edge of the pier. It was a magnificent structure, the pods large and made of glass, offering an unparalleled view of the park and the ocean beyond.

"It's like flying," Kade said as we approached the Ferris wheel. The ride was lit up in soft, glowing lights that reflected off the water below. "But it's even better when you're doing it with someone like me."

We stepped into one of the private pods, the door closing behind us with a soft click. The glass walls provided an almost panoramic view of the world outside, the lights and people below becoming distant as the ride began to ascend. The pod was spacious, with a bench along one side, but there was no mistaking the intimate atmosphere that surrounded us.

As the wheel slowly turned, lifting us higher into the night, Kade moved behind me, his hands sliding over my hips. He bent me over, my palms pressing against the cool glass as I looked out at the world below. I could see the people milling about, completely unaware of what was about to happen above them.

Kade's hand came down on my ass with a sharp

smack, the sting of it sending a jolt of pleasure straight to my core. I gasped, the sound echoing softly in the enclosed space, but instead of pulling away, I leaned into him, arching my back to offer myself to him completely.

"Fuck me," I whispered, the words coming out as a plea, raw with need.

Kade didn't need any more encouragement. He dropped to his knees behind me, his hands spreading my cheeks as he buried his face between them. His tongue lashed out, tasting me, teasing me, and I moaned, the sensation overwhelming. My body trembled as pleasure thrummed through me, every nerve ending alive with desire.

He licked and sucked, his tongue plunging into my pussy, driving me wild with each flick and caress. My fingers clawed at the glass, my breaths coming in ragged gasps as I pressed back against him, desperate for more.

"Please," I begged, my voice thick with need. "I need you inside me."

Kade stood, his shorts falling to the floor in one fluid motion. His cock was hard and throbbing, the sight of it sending another wave of arousal coursing through me. He positioned himself behind me, his hands gripping my hips as he slowly slid his thick length inside me.

I moaned, the feeling of him filling me to the brim, stretching me in ways that made my toes curl. I leaned back against him, taking every inch of him, my body trembling with the intensity of it.

Kade moved slowly at first, his cock sliding in and out of me with a steady rhythm that had me biting my lip to keep from crying out. Each thrust was harder, deeper, and my mind spun with the sensation of being so utterly possessed.

His hand moved to my breast, his fingers pinching and rubbing my nipple as he continued to fuck me. The pleasure built and built, coiling tight in my core, but just as I was on the edge of release, Kade pulled out, leaving me aching and desperate.

He sat down on the bench, his cock standing erect and ready. The Ferris wheel was nearing the top, the world beneath us a beautiful blur of lights and movement. Kade's eyes locked on mine, a challenge in his gaze.

"Come here," he commanded, his voice leaving no room for argument. "You have to come before the ride ends."

I straddled him, my legs trembling as I lowered myself onto his cock, taking him in all the way, until he was buried deep inside me. The feeling was indescribable, his length filling me completely as I began to move, riding him with a desperate need.

I kept my eyes locked on his, watching the way his expression shifted with each thrust, each roll of my hips. His hands gripped my waist, guiding me, but I was the one in control. I was the one taking what I wanted.

Kade leaned in, his lips brushing against my neck. "I wish you were a vampire," I whispered, my voice breathy and desperate. "I want to feel you drink my blood while I come, with the world watching."

His eyes flashed with something dark, something primal. "I can be whatever you want," he murmured against my skin, his teeth grazing the sensitive flesh of my neck.

And then he bit down.

The pain was sharp, but it quickly morphed into something else, something that had my entire body tightening with pleasure. I could feel the blood leaving my body, feel the way his cock throbbed inside me as he drank, and it was more erotic than anything I had ever imagined.

My orgasm hit me like a tidal wave, crashing over me with a force that left me gasping. My body shook, my vision blurred, and all I could do was cling to him as the pleasure consumed me, drowning me in its intensity.

I threw my head back, crying out as I came, my body trembling with the force of it. I could see the world below, the hungry eyes of every man and woman on the boardwalk fixed on us, and it only made the pleasure more intense. They were watching, they knew what we were doing, and I loved it.

Kade didn't stop, his teeth sinking deeper as he

continued to thrust into me, each movement sending another wave of pleasure through me. The feel of his mouth on my neck, his cock buried deep inside me, and the knowledge that we were being watched—it was all too much.

I came again, harder this time, my entire body tensing as the orgasm ripped through me. Kade growled against my neck, his hands tightening on my waist as he held me down, his cock pulsing inside me as he came with me, filling me with his release.

The world seemed to spin around us as we rode out the aftershocks together, our bodies entwined, our breaths ragged. When I finally opened my eyes, I looked out at the boardwalk, at the people who had witnessed our raw, primal passion.

They were still watching, their eyes wide with a mixture of awe and desire, and it made my blood sing with exhilaration.

Kade licked the wound on my neck, his tongue soothing the bite marks as he pulled me close, his arms wrapping around me in a possessive embrace. "You're mine now," he whispered against my ear, his voice rough with satisfaction. "And I'm never letting you go."

I smiled, the thrill of what we had just done still buzzing through me. "Good," I whispered back. "Because I don't want you to."

As the Ferris wheel began its descent, I leaned

against Kade, my body still trembling from the intensity of it all. The night was far from over, and I knew that whatever happened next, it would be just as unforgettable.

Because in this world, I was in control, and I intended to take everything I wanted.

And right now, I wanted more.

Chapter Five

The Ferris wheel slowly brought us back to the ground, but the adrenaline still buzzed in my veins. The exhilaration of what had just happened left me feeling both empowered and vulnerable. I leaned against Kade, feeling the warmth of his body against mine, the cool air brushing over our flushed skin.

As the pod door opened, I turned to Kade with a mischievous smile. "I want ice cream," I said, the simplicity of the request almost jarring after the intensity of the moments we'd just shared.

Kade chuckled, his eyes crinkling at the corners. "Ice cream it is. Any particular flavor?"

"Mint chocolate chip," I said without hesitation, already imagining the cool, creamy sweetness on my tongue. "And I want to sit on the dock with our feet in the ocean."

"That sounds perfect," Kade agreed, his hand warm in mine as he led us through the bustling amusement park. The bright lights and laughter felt like they were in another world compared to the private, intimate space we had just shared.

We found a small ice cream stand, the scent of freshly made waffle cones pulsed in the air. Kade ordered for us, and soon we were walking toward the dock, each of us with a cone in hand. The sun had moved, and we were in the early evening from the looks of it. The ocean waves gently lapped against the wooden beams as we made our way to the end of the pier.

We sat down, dangling our feet over the edge and dipping them into the cool water. The contrast of the chilly ocean against the warmth of Kade's presence was soothing, grounding me in the moment. I licked my ice cream, savoring the minty freshness, but my mind wandered, the earlier thrill giving way to deeper thoughts.

"I don't let many people into my life," I began, my voice quiet as I stared out at the horizon. "It's hard to imagine someone living alongside me, with everything that comes with my condition."

Kade was silent for a moment, his gaze steady as he listened. "It's understandable," he said finally. "Your condition is a part of who you are, but it doesn't define you. You're worthy of love, Clark. Just as you are."

I smiled, though it felt tinged with sadness. "You say that, but it's not just about being worthy. It's about the reality of living with someone like me. The restrictions, the fears… it's a lot to ask of anyone."

Kade turned slightly, his hand resting on mine. "You're right. It's not easy. But there are plenty of people who live with challenges, who find love and happiness despite them. Vampires, for instance—they've adapted, found ways to live successfully even with their own limitations."

I chuckled, shaking my head. "Vampires, huh? You really think I could live like one?"

He smiled, a thoughtful look in his eyes. "I think you could live however you choose."

A question hung in the air between us, heavy with possibility. "How long can I stay?" I asked, my voice barely above a whisper, the longing evident in my tone.

Kade's expression softened. "There are other places that would be more conducive to your needs. You mentioned vampires earlier. They're real, but not here. This isn't a long term place. This is a temporary space between realms."

His words made my heart skip a beat. "Other realms? Are you saying vampires are real? Like what?"

"There's the Shadow Realm," Kade explained, his voice taking on a more serious tone. "It exists side by side with the human realm. Coral Cove is located in a very special place where the worlds intersect, and magic is real. The Shadow Realm is a place where people like you could live without fear of the sun, where the night is your ally."

I stared at him, my mind racing. "And the other place?"

"The Fae Lands," Kade said, his eyes gleaming with a mixture of reverence and caution. "It's a place not unlike this one—born of desires and stories. If a story exists in the human world, it likely exists for real there. It's a place of beauty and danger, where the rules of reality are fluid, shaped by belief and imagination."

I shivered, the idea both thrilling and terrifying. "So, the fairy tales we grew up with… they're real there?"

Kade nodded. "In a way, yes. All stories that get told enough are born there. It's a place where belief gives life to dreams and nightmares alike."

My thoughts swirled, trying to grasp the enormity of what he was saying. "If I went there… would my desires be present like they are here in Coral Cove?"

Kade considered the question, his brow furrowing slightly. "I can't say for sure. The Fae Lands are unpredictable, and much of that world relies on belief. If you believe that you're safe, you will be. If you believe in your desires strongly enough, they may manifest. But the Shadow Realm…

it might be more aligned with your needs. You could stay who you are and find a world open to you."

"But it doesn't have the sun," I said softly, the realization settling over me like a heavy weight.

Kade's hand tightened around mine. "No, it doesn't. But it offers other freedoms. The choice is yours, Clark. You don't have to resign yourself to only what you've been told is possible."

I stared out at the ocean, the waves glistening under the moonlight. The idea of living in a world without the sun was both comforting and confining. I had lived in darkness for so long—was I really ready to accept that as my only reality?

"How would one find themselves in these other places?" I asked, my voice tinged with curiosity and a touch of fear.

"Ask Ms. Vesper," Kade said, his tone gentle. "She'll guide you. And if you decide to visit the Shadow Realm, look me up. But don't make any decisions based on anyone else's expectations. You've had to sacrifice your whole life, and the world is different now. You can do whatever you want, Clark."

His words hung in the air, a promise and a challenge all at once. I looked at Kade, his face bathed in the soft glow of the sun, and I realized that for the first time in a long time, I had a choice. A real choice.

The world was vast and full of possibilities, and for once, I didn't want to be limited by fear or by the constraints of my condition. I wanted to explore, to see what lay beyond the boundaries I'd been forced to accept.

But more than anything, I wanted to do it on my own terms.

As I sat there with Kade, the taste of mint chocolate chip ice cream lingering on my tongue, I made a silent vow to myself. Whatever I chose, it would be because it was what I wanted—not because it was what I was told was possible.

The evening was still young, and the future, for the first time in my life, felt wide open.

Chapter Six

The sun hovered low on the horizon, casting long shadows across the beach as the sky blazed in shades of orange and pink. It was the kind of sunset that made time seem to slow down, each moment stretching out with a breath-taking clarity. I stood with Kade, our feet still dipped in the cool ocean water, the ice cream long forgotten. My heart pounded with a mix of excitement and longing, knowing that our time in this dream world was nearing its end.

"Kade," I said, my voice barely above a whisper as I watched the sun sink lower. "There's one last thing I want to do before the sun sets."

He turned to me, his eyes filled with warmth and understanding. "Anything, Clark. Name it."

I took a deep breath, the idea already forming in my mind, daring and impossible, yet exactly what I needed. "I want to jump out of a plane. With a parachute, of course," I added with a grin. "Because of my XP, it's one of those things I can't even fathom doing. They don't let newbs jump out of planes at night—at least not around here."

Kade's smile widened, his expression a mix of admiration and amusement. "Your wish is my command."

And just like that, the world shifted. We were no longer on the beach, but boarding a small, sleek plane, the interior bathed in the golden glow of the setting sun. The engines roared to life, and the adrenaline coursed through my veins as I realized what I was about to do.

Kade turned to me, his hand gently cupping my face as he leaned in for a kiss. It was soft, tender, filled with all the emotions we hadn't yet put into words. When he pulled back, his eyes locked onto mine, serious but full of excitement.

"I'll show you which ropes to pull," he said, his voice steady and reassuring. "But are you sure, Clark? You don't have to do this if you're not ready."

I grinned, feeling more alive than I ever had in my entire life. "Hell yes, I'm sure. Let's do this."

He strapped the parachute onto my back, his hands lingering for just a moment longer than necessary, as if he was committing the feel of me to memory. He explained the process, his voice calm and methodical, pointing out which ropes to pull and when to deploy the chute. I nodded, absorbing every word, but there was no fear—only pure, unadulterated excitement.

The plane climbed higher, the world below growing smaller, the ocean a vast, shimmering expanse beneath us. The sky around us was painted in vivid hues, the last rays of the sun casting a golden light that made everything seem ethereal, almost dreamlike.

Then Kade opened the door, the rush of wind filling the cabin as he turned to me, his hand outstretched. "Ready?"

I took his hand, the connection between us grounding me in the moment. "Ready."

And then we jumped.

We plunged through the sky, the wind whipping around us, the sensation of weightlessness unlike anything I'd ever experienced. My heart raced, the exhilaration of freefalling a high all on its own. The sky was vast and endless, the sunset blazing around us as we descended, faster and faster, the ground rushing up to meet us.

I felt like I was flying, the world spinning and blurring, but I wasn't afraid. I was alive, more alive than I had ever been, and the thrill of it was pure ecstasy.

Kade was by my side the entire time, his presence a steadying force as we plummeted through the sky. When it was time, I pulled the cord, the parachute deploying with a satisfying whoosh, and our descent slowed to a gentle glide. The view was breathtaking, the beach and ocean laid out below us like a perfect postcard, the sunset casting everything in a warm, golden glow.

We floated down together, the experience almost surreal, as if the world had paused just for us. The sound of the waves grew louder as we approached the beach, the sand softening under our feet as we made a perfect, gentle landing right back where we had started.

Kade was immediately at my side, his hands deftly untangling me from the parachute ropes. But his touch didn't stop there. His fingers moved with purpose, unfastening the straps, and then he was peeling away my clothes, piece by piece, until I stood before him, completely exposed.

"I want you to make love to me," I whispered, my voice trembling with desire and something deeper, something almost sacred.

Kade's eyes darkened, his expression filled with a fierce intensity. "As you wish."

The blanket from earlier reappeared on the sand, soft and inviting, as Kade gently laid me down. He moved over me, his body pressing against mine as he kissed me, slow and deep, as if savoring every second. His lips trailed down my neck, across my collarbone, and lower still, leaving a burning trail of pleasure in their wake.

He worshiped every inch of my skin, his hands and mouth exploring, teasing, driving me wild with anticipation. When he finally entered me, it was with a slow, deliberate thrust, his cock filling me completely, the sensation overwhelming in the most exquisite way.

I gasped, my body arching up to meet his, the connection between us electric. Kade's movements were slow at first, his hips rolling as he drove deeper with each thrust, his eyes never leaving mine. The world around us seemed to disappear, the only thing that mattered was the way our bodies moved together, the way he made me feel.

The pleasure built steadily, each thrust sending waves of ecstasy rippling through me. Kade's hand slid down between us, his fingers finding my clit and circling it with expert precision, intensifying the sensation until I was teetering on the edge of bliss.

"Come for me, Clark," he whispered, his voice rough with need.

And I did. The orgasm tore through me, my entire body trembling as I screamed his name, the world blurring around us as the pleasure consumed me. Kade didn't stop, his fingers working in tandem with his thrusts, pushing me higher and higher until I shattered completely, lost in the sensation.

When it was over, he collapsed beside me, pulling me into his arms as the last rays of the sun dipped below the horizon. We lay there together, our bodies tangled, our breaths slowly evening out as the world returned to focus around us.

Kade held me close, his hand gently stroking my hair as the stars began to twinkle in the darkening sky. The warmth of his body against mine, the steady beat of his heart beneath my cheek, it was all so perfect, so right.

The lingering warmth of Kade's embrace still clung to my skin, but the comforting illusion of the Arcane Room was fading, replaced by the cold reality of my existence. The darkness outside loomed like a heavy curtain, a constant reminder of the life I was confined to—a life without the sun.

I pulled away from Kade, curling up on the edge of the lounge, my arms wrapped tightly around my knees. The silence between us was thick, and though I could feel Kade's eyes on me, I couldn't bring myself to meet his gaze.

"It's always like this," I whispered, my voice trembling with the raw emotion that clawed at my throat. "Every time I leave this place, it's like losing the sun all over again. I forget, just for a moment, what it feels like to be trapped in the dark, but then... reality comes crashing back."

Kade shifted beside me, his presence a steady, grounding force against the whirlwind of my thoughts. "Clark," he began softly, his hand reaching out to brush a strand of hair behind my ear. "The darkness isn't your enemy."

I turned my head slightly, catching a glimpse of his face in the dim light of the room. There was no pity in his eyes, only understanding—a depth of understanding that made my heart ache. "It's not fair," I said, the words escaping in a broken breath. "I'll never feel the sun on my skin, never see the world in daylight. It's like I'm only living half a life."

"That's not true," Kade replied, his tone firm but gentle. "You don't need the sun to live a full life. The darkness... it holds beauty too. There are things you can only see in the dark—things that are part of who you are."

I shook my head, tears welling up in my eyes. "Like what? What could possibly be worth missing out on the light?"

Kade cupped my face in his hands, forcing me to look at him. "Like the way you glow in the moonlight, the way your eyes sparkle when you're lost in the night. Like the way you move, so sure of yourself in the shadows. You are a part of the darkness, Clark. It isn't just something you endure; it's something you own."

I blinked, the tears spilling over as I struggled to find the words. "But it's lonely," I admitted, my voice barely a whisper. "The darkness is so lonely."

"It doesn't have to be," Kade said, his thumbs brushing away my tears. "You have me. And there are others—others who thrive in the night, who see the world in ways that daylight can't offer. The night is a place where anything is possible, where dreams and reality blur. You can find beauty in it, if you let yourself."

I wanted to believe him. I wanted to see the darkness as something more than just a void, something more than just a reminder of what I couldn't have. But the fear was still there, gnawing at the edges of my mind, making me doubt.

"What if I never see the sun again?" I asked, the question hanging in the air like a weight that couldn't be lifted.

Kade leaned in, his forehead resting gently against mine. "Then I'll show you the stars," he whispered. "I'll show you the beauty of the night sky, the constellations that tell stories older than time. I'll show you how the world comes alive in the dark—the creatures, the magic, the secrets that the sun hides away. I'll show you that the night can be just as full of life, just as full of love."

A shiver ran through me, not from fear, but from the realization that maybe, just maybe, Kade was right. Maybe the darkness wasn't something to be feared, but something to be embraced—a part of me that I had yet to fully understand.

I took a deep breath, letting Kade's words sink in, letting them wrap around my heart like a comforting blanket. "And what if I fall in love with the night?" I asked, my voice trembling with a mixture of hope and uncertainty.

Kade smiled, a soft, warm smile that made my heart flutter. "Then you'll find that it's not such a bad thing to love," he said. "Because in the darkness, you can be whoever you want to be. You can create your own light, your own warmth. You can find love, adventure, and endless possibilities—just like you did in the Arcane Room. And Clark, you are one of the reasons I love the darkness."

His words were cool water to my soul, soothing the ache that had been festering for so long. I looked into his eyes, seeing not just the man in front of me, but the possibilities he offered, the life he wanted to share with me—a life that wasn't bound by the sun.

For the first time, I let myself imagine a future without the sun, a future where the night was my ally, not my enemy. It was a scary thought, but as I sat there with Kade, his arms wrapped around me, I realized it was also a liberating one.

Maybe the darkness wasn't something I had to fight against. Maybe it was something I could learn to love.

"I think I'm ready," I said, my voice steady now, my resolve firm. "I'm ready to see the beauty in the dark."

Kade's smile widened, his eyes shining with pride and affection as he pulled me closer.

As the last bit of sunlight faded away completely, I felt a strange pull, a gentle tug that seemed to come from deep within. I blinked, the world around me shifting, the beach and the ocean dissolving into soft, blurred edges.

When I opened my eyes again, I was no longer on the beach. I was back in the Arcane Room, lying on the black leather chaise lounge. The room was quiet, the only sound was the soft ticking of a clock somewhere in the distance.

I sat up slowly, disoriented, my mind still lingering on the beach, on Kade's touch, on the sunset that had felt like it was ours alone.

Ms. Vesper stood in the doorway, a knowing smile on her lips. "Welcome back, Clark."

I looked around, the dreamlike quality of the experience still lingering. "Was it all just… a dream?"

Ms. Vesper's smile widened. "Not just a dream, my dear. A glimpse into what could be. The choices are yours to make."

I nodded slowly, the weight of her words settling over me. The world outside the Arcane Room was waiting, filled with possibilities I had never imagined. And now, for the first time in my life, I felt ready to face them.

But before I left, there was one thing I knew for sure—the sun might not be part of my reality, but love, adventure, and endless possibilities? Those were mine to claim.

And I intended to do just that.

Chapter Seven

The Arcane Room was as still and serene as ever, the soft light casting gentle shadows across the walls. Ms. Vesper watched me with those knowing eyes, her presence comforting and steady. I had just returned from a place that felt more real than reality itself, and yet here I was, back in the familiar space where it had all begun.

I took a deep breath, the weight of my thoughts pressing down on me. "Ms. Vesper," I began, my voice tentative. "I need to know more about the Fae and Shadow worlds. I need to understand what's possible... what's really out there."

Ms. Vesper nodded slowly, as if she had been expecting this. "The Fae world and the Shadow Realm are both very real, Clark. Each offers its own unique experiences and challenges. But before we delve into those, I want to remind you of something important."

I met her gaze, sensing the seriousness in her tone.

"Your life, Clark, is not over," she said gently. "Your condition may limit you in certain ways, but it doesn't define the entirety of your existence. There is still so much life left to live, and it's up to you to choose how you want to live it."

I swallowed hard, the truth of her words resonating deep within me. "I know," I whispered. "But I'm reaching the average age that someone with xeroderma pigmentosum lives to. I'm 26, Ms. Vesper. The average life span is around 30. And every time I mess up, every time I expose myself to the sun, I risk so much. Skin cancer, neurodegeneration… it's not just a risk, it's a certainty if I'm not careful. I don't want to die. I want to live."

Ms. Vesper's expression softened with understanding. "I know you do, my dear. And that's why it's so important for you to explore your options. Coral Cove is a special place, where the boundaries between worlds are thin. There is more to this town than meets the eye."

I leaned forward, eager to hear more. "You mentioned the Fae world. How can I find it?"

Ms. Vesper smiled, a hint of mischief in her eyes. "The entrance to the Fae world can be found at Lilly

Drake's Jewelry store. It's not something openly advertised, of course. Only those who are deemed the right fit are offered the opportunity to visit. The Fae world is beautiful, born of desires and stories, but it's also dangerous. It's a place where belief shapes reality, and not everything is as it seems."

Her words sent a shiver down my spine. "And the Shadow world? Is it... safer?"

"It's closer, in more ways than one," Ms. Vesper said thoughtfully. "The Shadow Realm exists alongside the human world, overlapping in places like Coral Cove. It wouldn't disrupt your life too much, and it might be more suited to your tastes and needs. It's a world of twilight, where the night is eternal, but it's not without its own risks."

I nodded, the weight of the decision settling over me. "Is there anything you recommend to help me make the decision?"

Ms. Vesper's eyes lit up, and she moved to one of the shelves, her hands deftly searching through the various items until she found what she was looking for. She returned with a small package, wrapped in delicate paper. "This is for you," she said, handing it to me.

I unwrapped the package, revealing a set of incense sticks. The scent was sweet and familiar, reminiscent of the pier and the time I had spent with Kade. "Cotton candy," I said with a smile, inhaling the comforting aroma.

Ms. Vesper nodded. "It's more than just a scent, Clark. These incense sticks will help you reflect on your time in the Arcane Room and decide what's best for you. There are only twenty in the pack, so use them sparingly. For the time it takes one to burn, you'll feel as if you're back in the Arcane Room, with a touch of sunlight on your skin. It's not quite the same, but it's a way to hold onto that feeling until you're ready to make your choice."

I felt a wave of gratitude wash over me. "Thank you, Ms. Vesper. This means more than you know."

She smiled, her eyes twinkling. "No decisions have to be made today, Clark. Take your time. Reflect on what you've experienced, and when you're ready, the path will be clear."

I nodded, clutching the incense package to my chest. "I will."

With a final nod of gratitude, I left the Arcane Room and headed home. The town was quiet, the streets bathed in the soft glow of streetlights. As I entered my house, I felt a sense of calm settle over me. I knew that my life had changed, that I had been given a glimpse of something extraordinary, and now it was up to me to decide how to move forward.

I lit the first incense stick, placing it in a holder on my nightstand. As the sweet, nostalgic scent filled the room, I felt a warmth spread across my skin, as if the sun itself had entered my little sanctuary. I closed my eyes, letting the sensation wash over me, imagining I was still in the Arcane Room, with Kade by my side.

It wasn't quite a decision, but it was helpful. For the length of time it took the incense to burn, I felt a connection to something greater, something beyond the limitations of my condition. I wasn't ready to decide yet, but I knew that I would use these incense sticks sparingly, as I considered my future.

Life had changed. The possibilities were endless, and for the first time in a long while, I felt like I had control over my destiny. Whatever I chose, it would be on my terms.

And that, more than anything, was a beginning.

CLARK AND KADE'S STORY CONTINUES IN THE FIRST book of the Costal Cupid series: *Hartbound Souls* .

SIGN UP FOR JAX WILDER'S NEWSLETTER AND RECEIVE A collection of unpublished Coral Cove short stories. Meet familiar characters and dive deeper into the love and romance that Coral Cove is known for. Don't miss out on this exclusive content!

https://mailchi.mp/158597581671/jax-wilder

Jax Wilder

Check out *The Perfect Lover Spell* in the Coral Cove series.

Accidental magic creates a perfect lover.

JESSA:

The love spell I cast was supposed to be a joke.

But now a Scotsman from 2014 is in my living room.

We must reverse the magic before he's stuck here forever.

But I'm falling for the perfect lover I never expected.

BRYCE:

One moment, I'm in Scotland; the next, I'm in Jessa's world.

This love spell has bound us together.

But can we break it before I lose my heart to the enchanting woman who summoned me?

A LOVE SPELL WITH UNEXPECTED RESULTS.

JESSA'S LOVE LIFE HAS BEEN A SERIES OF DISASTERS, FROM awkward dates to toxic relationships. Tired of swiping left and right, she's ready to give up on finding her perfect match. But when her best friend pushes her to try something different—a love spell from the mysterious Spellbound Stories bookstore—Jessa decides to take a chance on magic. Little does she know that casting The Perfect Lover Spell will bring more than she bargained for.

Enter Bryce MacGregor, a handsome and rugged Scotsman who literally appears out of nowhere... from ten years in the past. Struggling to make sense of his sudden time travel, Bryce must navigate modern-day Coral Cove while Jessa tries to reverse the spell. But as they spend more time together, the line between magic and reality blurs, and sparks begin to fly.

Can Jessa and Bryce find a way to break the spell without breaking their hearts? Or has fate—and a little magic—brought them together for a reason?

The Perfect Lover Spell is a steamy, time-travel

romance that blends humor, magic, and a sizzling connection that defies time itself. Perfect for fans of magical realism and heartwarming love stories.

Also by Jax Wilder

Coral Cove Series

Sleighed by Love

Harvesting Love

Dawning Desire

Knead You Now

Love Rewound

Perfect Lover Spell

Haunted by Her

Tarot Fantasies Series

The Devil's Temptations

Strength of the Beast

Hanged Passions

Six of Cups

Death's Embrace

Queen of Pentacles

Seven of Pentacles

Ace of Wands

Three of Swords

Two of Swords

Lovers In The Veil

Stand Alone Titles

Pride and Prejudice and Witches

Additional Books by

Rainbow Quartz Publishing Additional Titles:

MIRANDA LEVI

From A Youth A Fountain Did Flow

The Sea Withdrew

A Tear In Time

Mo(ther) Na(ture)

In Orion's Hands

Jackson Anhalt

From The 911 Files

LORELAI HAMILTON

Find Your Bliss

Teenage Witch's Grimoire

Tarot Reflection Journal

Tarot Refection Journal Coloring The Tarot

The Eclectic Witch's Grimoire

Dream Journal

Teenage Tarot

Tarot Tales and Magic Spells

Arcane In Verse

ISLA WATTS: A FAIRY BAD DAY

Surprise! You're a Vampire

Gorgeous, Gorgeous, Gorgons

Mork The Handsome Orc

Adopted By Werewolves

Bite Me If You Can

That's The Spirit!

ROSE DAWSON'S BOOK JOURNALS: MY TIME WITH THE FAIRIES

Enchanted Escapades

Enchanted Escapades

Dewey Decimal Diaries

Siren's Songbook

Pride and Prejudice

Bibliophile's Bounty

Book of Books Journal

Pages & Passages Reading Journal

Bookworm's Companion Reading Journal & Tracker

About the Author

Jax Wilder is a passionate romance author hailing from a charming small town nestled in the picturesque Pacific Northwest. With a heart full of love and an unyielding belief in the power of happily ever afters, Jax weaves enchanting tales of love and connection that leave readers captivated.

Jax's novels are a reflection of her commitment to celebrating the magic of love, and her characters' journeys mirror the warmth and happiness she has found in her own life. Join her on the enchanting journey of love, passion, and enduring connection through her heartfelt romance novels.